First published in Great Britain in 2017 by Pat-a-Cake
This edition published 2019
Copyright © Hodder & Stoughton Limited 2017. All rights reserved
Pat-a-Cake is a registered trade mark of Hodder & Stoughton Limited
ISBN: 978 1 52638 268 9 • 10 9 8 7 6 5 4 3 2 1
Pat-a-Cake, an imprint of Hachette Children's Group,
Part of Hodder & Stoughton Limited
Carmelite House, 50 Victoria Embankment, London EC4Y 0DZ
An Hachette UK Company
www.hachette.co.uk • www.hachettechildrens.co.uk
Printed in China

My Very First Story Time

Goldilocks
and the Three Bears

Retold by Ronne Randall

Illustrated by Tim Budgen

cottage

Daddy
Bear

Mummy
Bear

Baby
Bear

big bed

tiny bed

Daddy Bear's
porridge

middle-sized
bed

Mummy Bear's
porridge

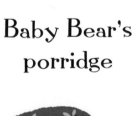

Baby Bear's
porridge

big chair

tiny chair

middle-sized chair

Once upon a time, there were three bears. Great big Daddy Bear, middle-sized Mummy Bear, and teeny-tiny Baby Bear. They always had porridge for breakfast.

One morning, their porridge was much too hot, so
the three bears went out for a walk while it cooled down.

A little girl called Goldilocks was walking through the woods, too. When she came to the three bears' cottage, she peeped in through the open window.

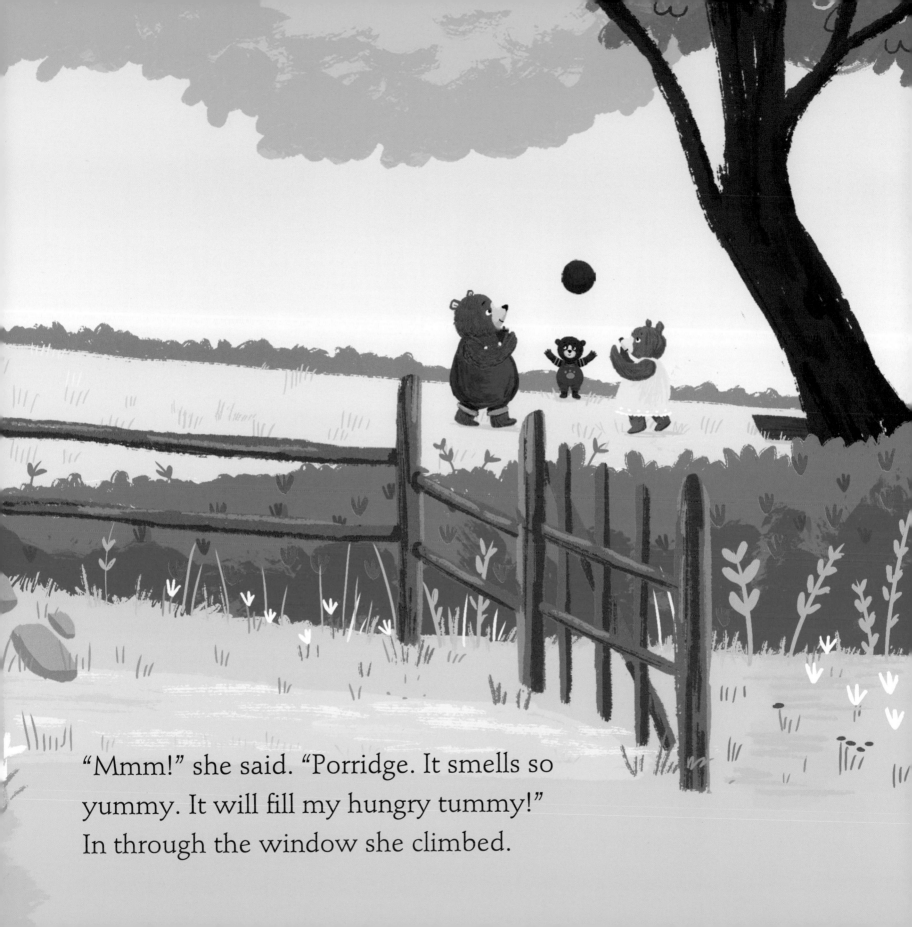

"Mmm!" she said. "Porridge. It smells so
yummy. It will fill my hungry tummy!"
In through the window she climbed.

Goldilocks tasted Daddy Bear's porridge. "Yuk!" she said. "Too salty!"

Next, she tried Mummy Bear's porridge. "Yuk!" she said. "Too sweet!"

Last of all, she tried Baby Bear's porridge.
"Mmm!" she said. "Just right!" She ate it
all up, right to the very last drop.

Goldilocks tiptoed further into the cottage and spied three chairs. "I think I'll sit down," she said.

The great big chair was so hard she jumped straight off.

The middle-sized chair was so soft she got stuck.

The teeny-tiny chair looked just right. But when Goldilocks sat on it, CRACK! It fell to pieces.

Goldilocks was feeling more and more curious, so up the stairs she went. There were three beds, and she tried them all. The great big bed was too high.

The middle-sized bed was too low.

But the teeny-tiny bed felt just right.
Goldilocks lay down and fell
fast asleep.

Soon, the three bears came home for their breakfast.

"Someone's been eating my porridge!" growled Daddy Bear.

"And someone's been eating my porridge!" said Mummy Bear.

"Someone's been eating my porridge and has eaten up every last drop!" cried Baby Bear.

The three bears looked at their chairs.
"Someone's been sitting in my chair!"
growled Daddy Bear.

"And someone's been sitting in my chair!"
said Mummy Bear.

"Someone's been sitting in my chair and has
broken it all to pieces!" cried Baby Bear.

The three bears marched upstairs.
"Someone's been sleeping in my bed!"
growled Daddy Bear.

"And someone's
been sleeping in
my bed!" said
Mummy Bear.

"Someone's been sleeping in my bed and she's still here!" cried Baby Bear.

All the noise woke Goldilocks.
What a fright she had when
she saw the three bears
standing over her!

"Oh!" she cried.
"Oh! Oh! Oh!"

Goldilocks jumped up, scampered downstairs, and went as fast as she could out of the three bears' house. She never went back again.

And the three bears never again left their window open when they went for a walk in the woods.

Point to the teeny-tiny bear.

Point to the middle-sized chair.

Point to the biggest bowl.

Which bear will go to sleep in which bed?

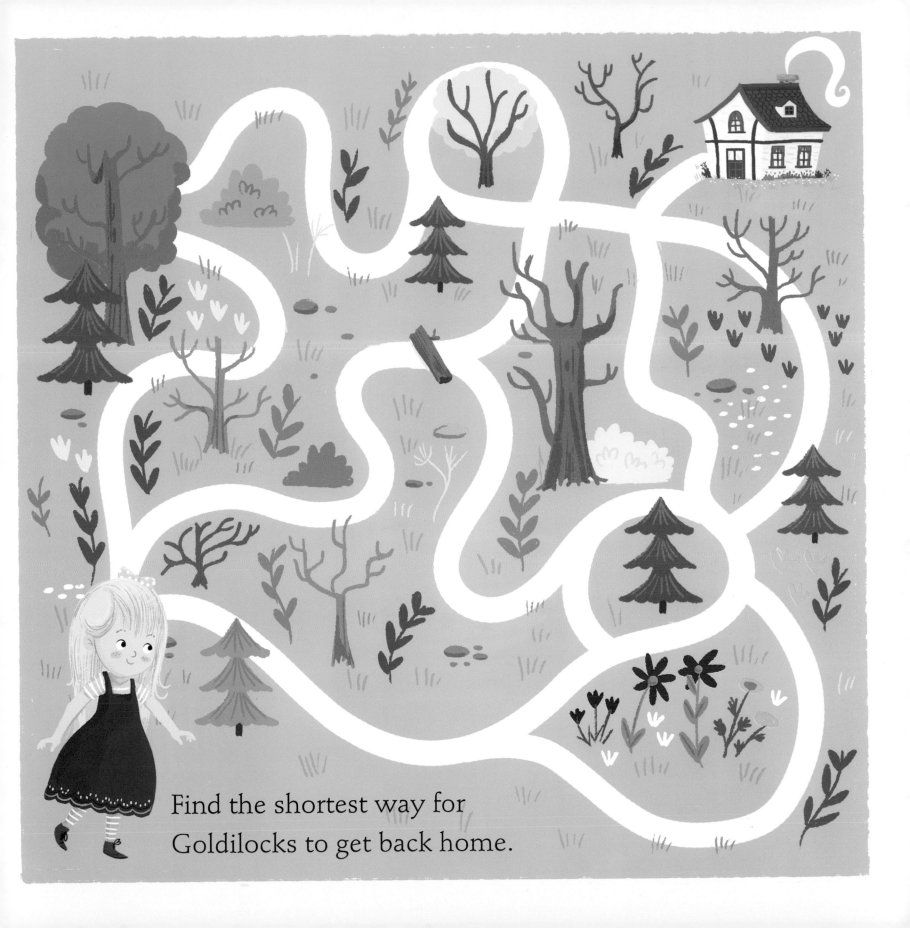

Find the shortest way for Goldilocks to get back home.